CoComelon™

I LIKE SCHOOL!

Adapted by Maggie Testa
Ready-to-Read

SIMON SPOTLIGHT

An imprint of Simon & Schuster Children's Publishing Division • New York London Toronto Sydney New Delhi
1230 Avenue of the Americas, New York, New York 10020 • This Simon Spotlight edition May 2023
CoComelon™ & © 2023 Moonbug Entertainment. All Rights Reserved. • All rights reserved, including
the right of reproduction in whole or in part in any form. SIMON SPOTLIGHT, READY-TO-READ, and
colophon are registered trademarks of Simon & Schuster, Inc. • For information about special discounts for
bulk purchases, please contact Simon & Schuster Special Sales at 1-866-506-1949
or business@simonandschuster.com.
Manufactured in the United States of America 0323 LAK • 10 9 8 7 6 5 4 3 2 1
ISBN 978-1-6659-3140-3 (hc) • ISBN 978-1-6659-3139-7 (pbk) • ISBN 978-1-6659-3141-0 (ebook)

Here is a list of all the words you will find in this book. Sound them out before you begin reading the story.

Word families:

"-ay"	→	play	today
"-ool"	→	cool	school
"-ook"	→	book	look

Sight words:

going	in	is	like	our
these	this	to	we	what
will	with			

Bonus words:

blocks	colors	learn	letters
music	numbers	pretend	shapes
toys			

Ready to go? Happy reading!

Don't miss the questions about the story
on the last page of this book.

JJ is going to school today.

We like school!

What will we learn?

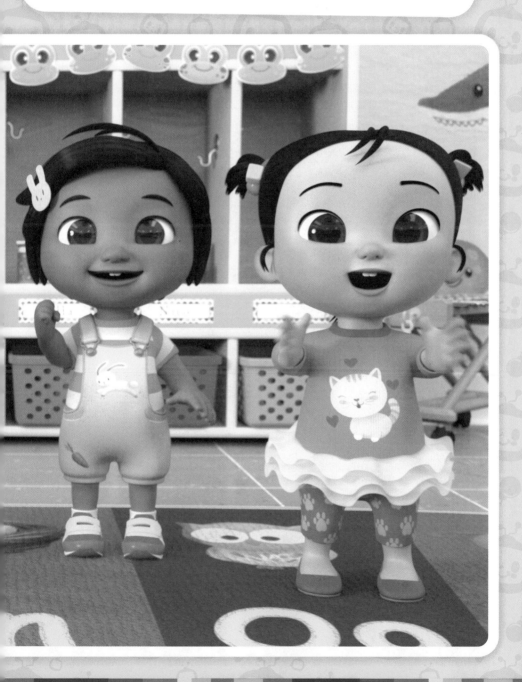

We look in this book.

We learn our letters.

We learn these shapes.

We learn these colors.

What will we play?

We play with toys!

We play with blocks!

We play music!

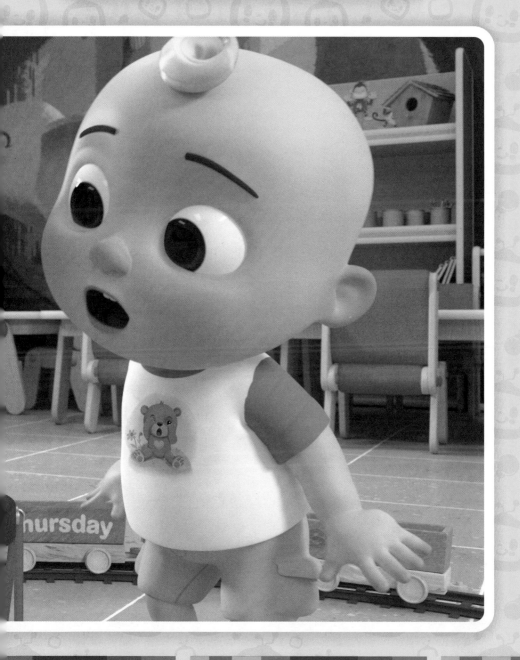

We play pretend!

School is cool!

We like school!

Now that you have read the story, can you answer these questions?

1. What do you like to do at school? If you do not go to school yet, what kinds of things are you looking forward to doing when you do go?

2. What is your favorite book to read?

3. In this book you read the words "cool" and "school." Those words rhyme! Can you think of other words that rhyme with "cool" and "school"?

Great job!
You are a reading star!